WITHDRAWN

DATE DUE

DEMCO

SEAS AND OCEANS

The POLAR SEAS

Malcolm Penny

RSVP

RAINTREE
STECK-VAUGHN
PUBLISHERS
The Steck-Vaughn Company

Austin, Texas

Seas and Oceans series

The Atlantic Ocean
The Caribbean and the Gulf of Mexico
The Indian Ocean
The Mediterranean Sea
The North Sea and the Baltic Sea
The Pacific Ocean
The Polar Seas
The Red Sea and the Arabian Gulf

Cover: A small fishing boat, dwarfed by icebergs in Jakobshavn, West Greenland

Published by Raintree Steck-Vaughn Publishers, an imprint of Steck-Vaughn Company

Library of Congress Cataloging-in-Publication Data
Penny, Malcolm.
The polar seas / Malcolm Penny.
 p.   cm.—(Seas and oceans)
Includes bibliographical references and index.
Summary: Examines the geography, plants, animals, trade, and resources of the polar seas.
ISBN 0-8172-4513-8
1. Arctic Ocean—Juvenile literature.
2. Antarctic Ocean—Juvenile literature.
[1. Arctic Ocean. 2. Antarctic Ocean.]
I. Title. II. Series: Seas and oceans (Austin, Tex.)
GC401.P46   1997
551.46'8—dc20   96-27732

Printed in Italy. Bound in the United States.
1 2 3 4 5 6 7 8 9 0 01 00 99 98 97

Picture acknowledgments:
Bryan & Cherry Alexander *cover*, 14 (Paul Drummond), 18 (David Rootes), 19 (David Rootes), 20, 21, 22, 23, 28–29, 30 (Julian Dowdeswell), 34, 35, 40 (NASA); Dieter Betz 4–5, 13 (bottom), 15, 16 (bottom), 29 (top); British Antarctic Survey 33 (D. Stewart), 44 (M. R. A. Thomson); Ecoscene 16 (top/Robert Weight), 17 (Whittle), 27 (Stuart Donachie), 36–37 (Farmer), 38–39 (both), 41 (Robert Weight); Mary Evans Picture Library 24, 25, 26; Frank Lane Picture Agency 9 (C. Carvalho), 31 (both/S. McCutcheon), 36 (W. Wisniewski), 37 (top/W. Wisniewski), 45 (E. and D. Hosking; Science Photo Library 7 (Tom Van Sant/Geosphere Project); Tony Stone Worldwide 12 (Joel Bennett), 13 (top/John Beatty), 42 (bottom left/Alan Levenson), 42–43 (top/Fred Felleman).
All artwork is produced by Hardlines except Peter Bull 4 (bottom), 5 (top), 21 (left), 32.

Contents

Words that appear in **bold** in the text can be found in the glossary on page 46.

INTRODUCTION
At Opposite Ends of the Earth

The Arctic Ocean in the north, and the Antarctic Ocean in the south, look very similar at first sight, and they have a lot in common. But they also differ in many ways. Both are partly covered by ice. But the Arctic Ocean is mainly water surrounded by land, while the Antarctic is a ring of water surrounding the world's fifth-largest continent—Antarctica.

The ancient Greeks gave the Arctic its name, from the **constellation** known to them as the Great Bear (the Greek for bear is *arktos*), which appeared to revolve around the North Pole. Believing that there must be a pole at the other end of the world, they called this the "anti-Arctic." By coincidence, there are bears in the Arctic, but not in the Antarctic.

The boundaries of each ocean can be fixed in different ways. The polar regions can be defined as the limits of the

Below left: The Arctic Ocean is a relatively shallow basin, connected with the rest of the world's oceans by channels between the landmasses that surround it.

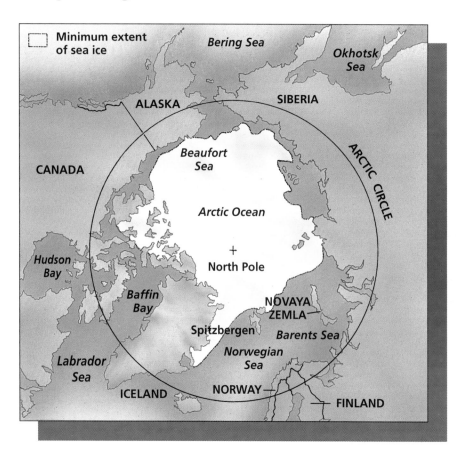

Right: The boundary of the Antarctic Ocean is outside the Antarctic Circle, just enclosing the islands of South Georgia.

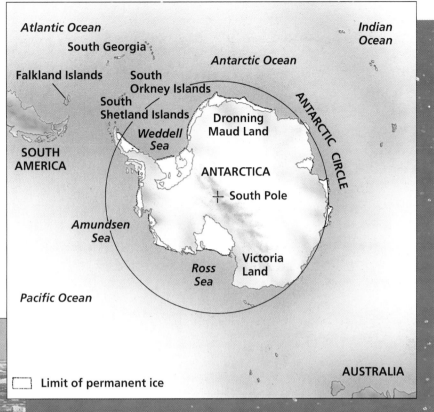

Atlantic Ocean

South Georgia

Falkland Islands

South Orkney Islands

South Shetland Islands

Weddell Sea

SOUTH AMERICA

Indian Ocean

Antarctic Ocean

ANTARCTIC CIRCLE

Dronning Maud Land

ANTARCTICA

+ South Pole

Amundsen Sea

Victoria Land

Ross Sea

Pacific Ocean

AUSTRALIA

☐ Limit of permanent ice

Below: The icy waters of the polar seas look barren, but they support a rich food chain under their forbidding surface.

Midnight Sun—that is, places where, on at least one day in the year, the sun does not set. The **astronomical** Polar Circles are 66.5° north and south of the equator. The geographical boundaries are defined in a different way. The Arctic Ocean, lying well inside the Arctic Circle, is the area of water enclosed by the lands of North America, Eurasia, and Greenland. The Antarctic Ocean stretches beyond the Antarctic Circle. Its boundary is usually taken as the northern limit of the Antarctic Circumpolar Current, at about 53° south.

The polar waters are very different in human terms. People have lived around the shores of the Arctic Ocean for thousands of years, whereas the Antarctic has no permanent human inhabitants. The polar regions are important because their cold waters affect the **climate** of the whole Earth.

PHYSICAL GEOGRAPHY
The Arctic Ocean Floor

The Arctic Ocean is the world's smallest ocean. It is almost completely surrounded by land, so warmer currents from the south cannot reach its waters. It is for this reason that most of the Arctic Ocean is covered by ice year-round.

The world's oceans were not always the shape that they are now. Whole continents have moved and broken away from each other over millions of years. The Arctic Ocean is made up of two basins, which opened separately as the **plates** of the earth's surface drifted apart about 100 million years ago. The Eurasian Basin was formed when the sea floor spread along the line of a range of underwater mountains called the Nansen **Cordillera**, which is the northernmost part of the

Below: The two main basins of the Arctic Ocean are divided by the Lomonsov Ridge, which was once attached to Asia, but now lies under the North Pole.

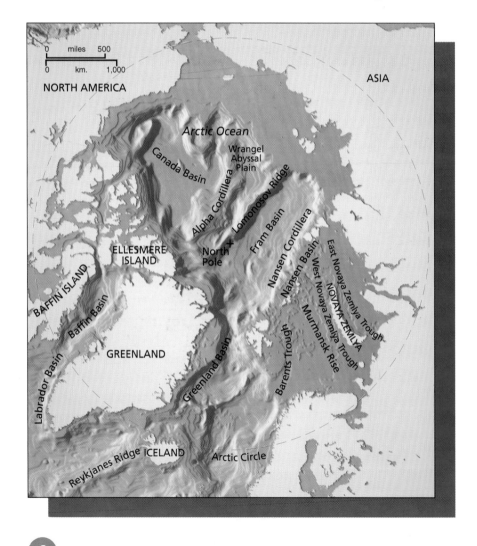

ASIA

NORTH AMERICA

miles 500

km. 1,000

Arctic Ocean

Wrangel Abyssal Plain

Canada Basin

Alpha Cordillera

Lomonosov Ridge

Fram Basin

Nansen Cordillera

Nansen Basin

East Novaya Zemlya Trough

West Novaya Zemlya Trough

NOVAYA ZEMLYA

Murmansk Rise

ELLESMERE ISLAND

North Pole

BAFFIN ISLAND

Baffin Basin

Labrador Basin

GREENLAND

Greenland Basin

Barents Trough

Reykjanes Ridge ICELAND

Arctic Circle

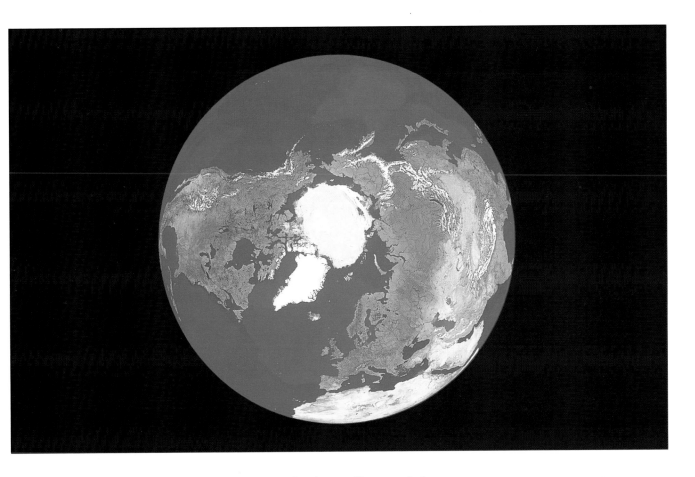

Mid-Atlantic Ridge. The movement pushed a splinter of the Asian continent away from the mainland. This fragment, the Lomonosov Ridge, now lies directly under the North Pole. At about the same time, the land that is now Alaska swung away from the rest of North America, leaving a hole known as the Canada, or Amerasian Basin, on the other side of the ridge.

Above: This satellite picture shows the Arctic Ocean area, covered by a pale blue, permanent ice cap. The land-masses of Eurasia, North America, and Greenland surround the ocean.

Sediments from **core samples** taken from below the ocean floor contain fossils that show that before about 40 million years ago, the water was warm. Sediments that sank to the ocean floor during the last 3 million years contained rock particles carried by the sea ice from glaciers around its shores. This means that for at least that time, the Arctic Ocean has been very cold, but no one has yet found out when the change took place.

How big and how deep?	
Arctic Ocean	
Area	5,440,000 sq. mi.
Average depth	3,300 ft.
Maximum depth	18,000 ft.

Around the Eurasian Basin, the **continental shelf** is very wide, between 300 and 1,100 miles, compared with the 60 to 125 miles around the Amerasian Basin. This amount of shallow water might account for the slightly warmer currents that keep the Eurasian shore free from ice for part of the year, making it an important shipping route.

The Antarctic Ocean Floor

The movements of the earth's crust that created the Antarctic Ocean were more recent than those that created the Arctic, although the Antarctic may have become frozen earlier. The Antarctic Ocean did not so much open as close. About 80 million years ago, during what geologists call the Cretaceous Period, there was a narrow gap full of seawater between Antarctica and Australia. This was a warm, shallow sea, linked to others in the hollows under what are now the **icecaps** of Lesser Antarctica. As the continents drifted farther apart, 28 million years ago, the Drake Passage opened between the Antarctic Peninsula and South America. Deep, cold water began to flow round the continent, forming the Antarctic Circumpolar Current. This enormous body of moving water cut off the Antarctic Ocean from warmer waters farther north, and the whole area began to freeze.

Right: The Ross Ice Shelf, seen from the sea. In 1956 the biggest iceberg ever seen, 12,000 sq. mi. in extent, broke off and drifted away to the north.

Below: The floor of the Antarctic Ocean is a deep, circular trough, cutting off the waters from the rest of the world's oceans.

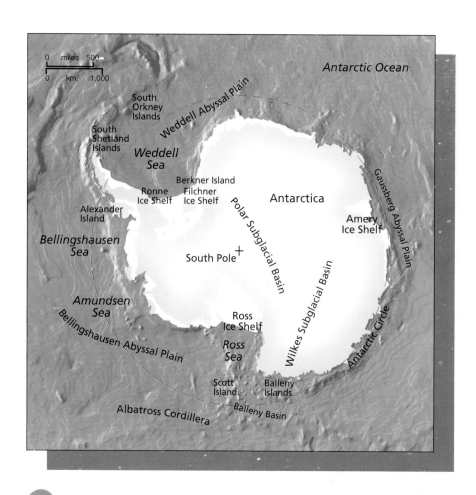

This may have been the time when the Arctic froze, as part of a worldwide pattern of changing climate, but proof of this has not yet been found.

The Antarctic ice cap contains nine-tenths of all the ice on Earth, locking up seven-tenths of all the freshwater. The Ross Ice Shelf, 230 ft. thick, covers an area of sea the size of France. Every winter, the area of pack ice, or sea ice, increases from its summer average of 1.5 million sq. mi. to 8 million sq. mi. So in winter the size of the Antarctic ice blanket grows from 7 to 13 million sq. mi.

How big and how deep?	
Antarctic Ocean	
Area	13,510,000 sq. mi.
Average depth	about 6,500 ft.
Maximum depth	over 16,400 ft.

When the pack ice melts again in summer, it forms a layer of relatively fresh water about 328 ft. deep, just below the surface. This water contains plenty of oxygen. As this water drifts away from the land, it gradually becomes colder and sinks, finally spreading through the oceans of the Southern Hemisphere.

Currents in Polar Waters

In the Arctic Ocean, the main movement of water, or current, is through the Fram Strait, a deep channel between Svalbard and Greenland. Water flows in from the Pacific through the Bering Strait, partly driven by wind, but partly because of a small difference in sea level. Rivers flow in from Canada, Alaska, and Siberia. Cold water flows south through the Fram Strait, diving to the bottom of the North Atlantic, where it has a marked effect on the temperature of the world's oceans and on the Earth's climate.

Adrift in the ice

The Canadian Arctic Expedition set sail in the summer of 1913 in the *Karluk*, a wooden ship with sails and a small steam engine. In October the explorers were trapped in the ice off northern Alaska, and by early January they found themselves off the coast of Siberia. They got off the ship just before it sank. Stranded on the ice were twenty-two men, one woman and her two children, sixteen dogs, and the ship's cat. Fortunately, the woman was an **Inuit**. With her family, she advised the others how to survive the Arctic winter. They reached Wrangel Island with the aid of the dog teams, and camped there while the captain and another Inuit man reached the Siberian mainland. Four other men died, but in September 1914, the rest of the expedition was rescued, including the cat.

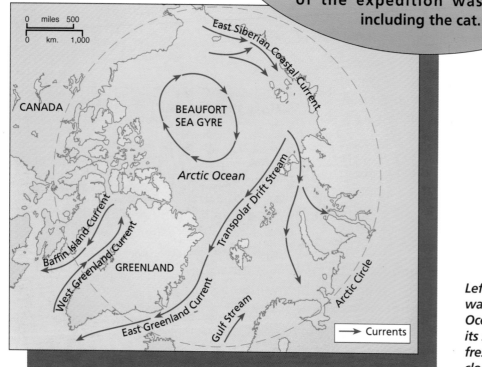

Left: About 2 percent of the water flowing into the Arctic Ocean is fresh, from rivers around its shores. The main currents mix freshwater and saltwater in a clockwise direction.

The main movement of surface water in the Arctic Ocean is to the west, (clockwise if seen from above). Within this pattern, there is a large, clockwise **gyre** in the Amerasian Basin, and some smaller, counterclockwise gyres among the islands and shallow water of the Eurasian Basin. A floating ice island in the Amerasian gyre completed two laps in twenty years.

The Antarctic Circumpolar Current is the world's largest body of moving water. From 125 to 600 miles wide, it flows at 4.5 billion cu. ft. per second, more than 400 times the volume of the Mississippi River. Strong winds from the west drive it eastward for 15,000 miles around the world. Seen from above, it circles the continent clockwise. Closer to land, the East Wind Drift moves along the shore in the opposite direction.

Where the Antarctic Polar Front meets the warm, southward-moving waters of the Indian, Pacific, and Atlantic oceans, cold water sinks to the bottom and spreads over the ocean floor. This Antarctic bottom water, which is very rich in oxygen, is the coldest and densest water on Earth. It cools more than half the world's oceans to less than 35°F.

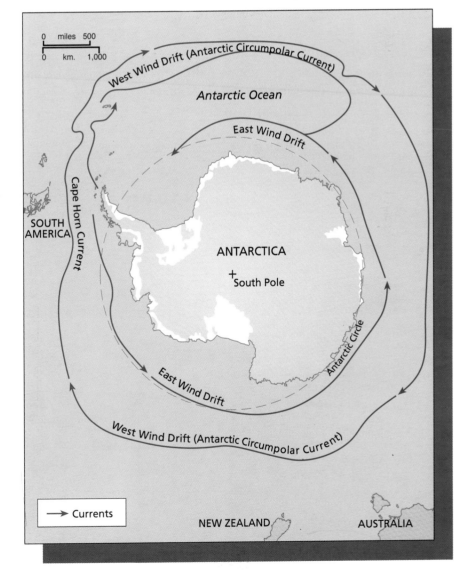

Right: The Antarctic Ocean is dominated by the Circumpolar Current, four times the size of the Gulf Stream in the Atlantic Ocean.

Ice Sheets and Icebergs

Sea ice is common to the polar seas. Floating on the surface, sea ice, or pack ice, prevents waves from mixing the water layers, and by reflecting sunshine it keeps the sun from warming the water. As seawater freezes, the salt is driven out as brine, creating a very cold, salty layer just under the ice. This supercooled water sinks, eventually joining the dense, cold water that flows out under the rest of the world's oceans. Newly frozen sea ice tastes salty—it contains about 30 percent seawater. After a year, the **salinity** drops by half, and the ice can be used for drinking. By this time it is about 7 ft. thick, and very hard. Sailors call it "polar pack." After two years or more, when it is 14 ft. thick, the ice is almost completely free from salt.

Pack ice moves with the ocean swell, opening cracks called "leads." It can rise to form peaks, called pressure ridges, and it often breaks and slides over itself, forming stacks several feet high. In some places, movements of wind and water

Right: When pack ice breaks up in summer, it drifts away from the North and South poles as ice floes.

Below: When they first break free, icebergs stand tall in the water. As this new iceberg begins to melt below the water line, it will roll over and change its shape.

create polynyas—open areas where ice does not form. Polynyas are often quite small, but they may be as large as 62 mi. wide. Along the Antarctic coastline, where offshore winds create many polynyas, they function as "ice factories." New ice formed on their surface is quickly blown out to sea. The open water of a polynya may be the only access to air for some far-ranging marine mammals.

Icebergs are formed on land, from tightly packed snow. They come from glaciers—rivers of ice creeping toward the sea— where each floats out as an ice shelf. Eventually, tides or waves cause pieces of ice to break off and float away. Icebergs may be as large as 152 mi. long and 68 mi. wide. They are 80 percent submerged underwater, and as they drift into warmer water, they are gradually melted from below and weathered from above by wind and rain. They may roll over many times before they finally melt away.

Below: A glacier tumbles toward the sea, carrying with it particles of rock from the shore.

	Arctic	Antarctic
Temperature Range	33 to 31°F	32 to 29°F
Salinity	28–35 parts/thousand	28 parts/thousand

Plants and Invertebrates

The seashores and shallow seas of polar regions can be very difficult places for plants and animals to live. Thick ice cover can block out the light that plants need to survive. Where the ice is thinner, tiny plants can live attached to the underside of the ice. These plants provide the food for a whole community of tiny animals that live upside down on the bottom of the ice.

The seashore and seabed in shallow water can be scraped bare by moving ice, making it almost impossible for animals to live there. But deeper, beyond the reach of grinding ice, there is an amazing variety of life. Among bright anemones and sea squirts live worms, prawns, sea urchins, and gigantic sea lice and sea spiders that are never seen in warmer waters.

In the polar waters, cold-blooded animals live their lives at a slower pace. Some of them manage to live for a very long time, sometimes growing to a "giant" size. One species of Antarctic limpet can live at least 100 years, and some sponges in cold waters survive for several centuries.

Below: Slow-moving and slow-living, an Antarctic starfish may live many times longer than its relatives in warmer waters.

The long, dark, polar winter is a difficult time for plants and for the animals that eat the plants. When summer comes, the tiny plant **plankton** around the ice edge and below the thinner ice start growing and multiplying, and others drift in from the open ocean. With them come the animal plankton that eat them. The main type of animal plankton are shrimplike creatures that are called **krill**, 2 or 3 in. long, which multiply into schools up to several miles wide, numbering many billions of individuals. In winter, krill feed on algae under the ice. When they are most plentiful in summer, all the krill of the polar waters together weigh about 650 million tons. The entire human race weighs about 100 million tons.

In the brief Arctic summer, the land is covered in flowering plants. They have to produce seeds in the few weeks before the cold closes in again.

Bear Pole, Bird Pole

The land **ecosystems** of the North and South poles are completely different. The shores of the Arctic Ocean support a variety of **mammals**, with **predators,** such as polar bears, wolves, and foxes, and **prey** animals, such as caribou, musk oxen, and Arctic hares.

In the Arctic, ringed seals and harbor seals are the most numerous species, but they eat fish rather than mammals, birds, or krill. The seal's main predator is the polar bear, a land animal whose prey comes mostly from the sea. The ringed seal defends itself against polar bears by giving birth in a chamber under the snow, reached from underneath through a hole in the ice. The other distinctive mammal of the Arctic is the walrus, which lives only in the Arctic Ocean and the nearby ice-covered seas.

The only land animals found in the Antarctic are tiny mites and **springtails**. In the south, marine mammals, such as elephant seals, were heavily exploited by humans until they became too scarce to be worth hunting. There, too, the

Above: Emperor penguins and their chicks at Halley Bay. Before the chicks hatched, the eggs were kept warm through the dark winter. They were incubated on the male penguin's feet, to keep them off the ice.

Left: Walruses move around the Arctic Ocean by drifting on ice floes. These walruses have hauled themselves onto land to bask in the sun.

A female Weddell seal about to give birth in the first sunlight of the Antarctic spring

leopard seal is a large, fierce predator of other mammals and birds, and the crabeater seal, in spite of its name, is the main krill-eater. Antarctic seals have no predators out of the water. Both polar regions have populations of fur seals, recovering after centuries of human persecution.

In the sea, the Arctic and Antarctic systems are more similar. Both have whales and dolphins, including the killer whale or orca, the most widely distributed predator in the world. Apart from the bowhead whale, found only in the Arctic Basin, all the other large **baleen** whales and the sperm whale are found in both polar oceans, and in all other waters between.

The bird life of the two oceans is very different. Both have skuas, gulls, and terns, but the Antarctic has huge populations of penguins, and large, mostly increasing, populations of albatrosses. These Antarctic birds depend on an abundant supply of krill and squid.

The first seal of spring

The only seal that can breed before the end of the Antarctic winter is the Weddell seal, which comes close to land in late August, when the shore ice is still 6.5 ft. thick. Females grind away at a crack in the ice with specially adapted front teeth, to make a hole big enough to climb through. They give birth on the ice, sheltering their pups from the wind with their bodies. By the time other seals arrive, the Weddell pups are swimming well, better able to escape predators such as leopard seals when they come in from the open ocean later in the year.

An Antarctic Problem: The Krill Equation

Although krill is plentiful throughout the Antarctic Ocean, the supply is not limitless. Animals that feed on krill must compete for their share. It appears that human interference has upset the delicate balance.

By the late 1950s, as a result of human hunting, Antarctic baleen whales reached their lowest population level. Several other changes in animal populations were noticed around this time. Fur seals, which had been almost wiped out by sealing in 1900, began to show signs of a remarkable recovery.

Below: The southern right whale is a major consumer of krill. But there may not be enough food for its population to recover from the large numbers that were killed when whaling was still common.

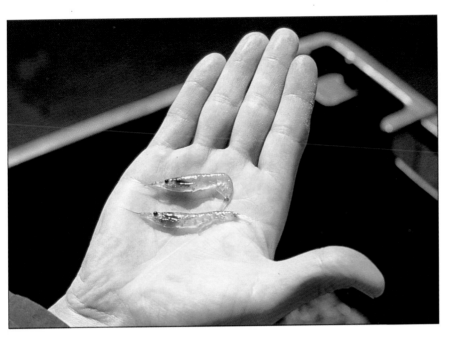

Krill is the basis of a huge food chain. If humans find a way to fish for large amounts of krill, they may deprive many polar animals of food. The reduced krill population would have a domino effect, and there would be a decrease in the numbers of the animals that depend on krill for food.

On Bird Island, near South Georgia, a group of thirty seals discovered in 1930 had increased to thousands by the late 1950s—by 1980, they numbered more than a million. At the same time, elsewhere in the Antarctic, macaroni penguins multiplied in numbers, and crabeater seals began to mature and breed nearly a year earlier than usual. All four species feed on krill.

Albatross numbers increased at the same time. They feed on squid, and squid feed on krill. All the signs pointed to a huge increase in the amount of available krill.

Scientists soon realized that extra krill had become available because the whales were not taking their share. They calculated that, before whaling began, the whale population would have needed about 100 million tons of krill per year. Although the summer krill population weighs about six times this amount, no one knows how much is produced each year, or how much can be taken without reducing the population. It seems that if the great whales are to recover, they will have to compete for food with the increased populations of fur seals, crabeater seals, squid, and penguins.

An added factor is human fishing for krill. At present this takes only about half a million tons per year, partly because it is hard to sell as human food, but the potential catch is huge. Solving the krill equation may be the key to the recovery of whales in the Antarctic.

Beyond the Tree Line

People have lived on the Arctic coast for thousands of years, using the resources of the land and the ocean. Their home is "beyond the **tree line**," too far north for agriculture, so they live mainly by hunting, trapping, and fishing.

People from south of the Arctic think of these far northern lands as barren and that those who live there endure a hostile climate. This is an outsider's view. To an Inuit from the coast, or an Aleut from the northernmost Pacific islands, their home is a comfortable place to live.

In winter, the Inuit and the Aleut hunt marine mammals on the frozen sea or catch fish through holes in the ice. Traditional hunting weapons include bows and arrows, harpoons, and spears, but today most northern hunters use rifles. Although marine mammals are protected from hunting by other people, natives of the Arctic can take what they need for food and clothing. Once, they hunted whales with harpoons from an umiak, a large open boat covered in skins. Modern transportation and communications make this dangerous method of getting food unnecessary today.

Right: A map showing the countries claiming territory in the Antarctic. One area has been claimed by the UK, Argentina, and Chile. In 1908, the UK made its first formal claim, which was renewed in 1913. Argentina claimed part of this territory in 1925, followed by Chile in 1940. Countries claiming territory in the Antarctic were hoping to be able to exploit the minerals in its rocks, but so far all mining has been banned.

Below: Opening the door to an igloo. Properly built, an igloo is a warm and comfortable place to sleep.

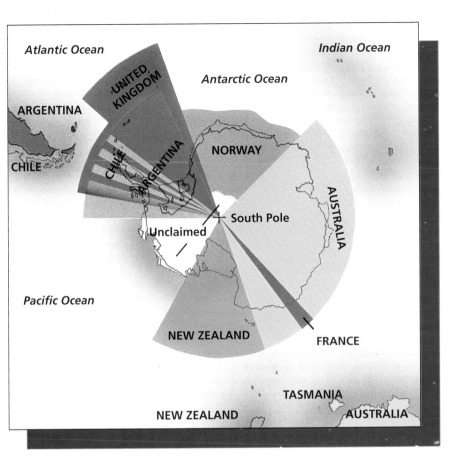

Above: Inuit people kill animals for food and clothing. This fisherman wears a coat made from the white fur of the Arctic fox.

In summer, the Inuit move inland to hunt on the **tundra** and to fish in its lakes and streams. There are wild berries, leaves, and roots to eat and a wide variety of animals. Some of their summer harvest can be stored for winter by drying or smoking the meat.

Aleut hunters stay at the coast, some of them still paddling sealskin kayaks to chase their prey, but most use modern fiberglass boats with **outboard motors**.

Inuit and Aleut villages today have schools and shops and people to work in them. But the main pattern of their lives is determined by where they live and the seasons of the year, each with its bounty to be gathered by those who know how.

Territorial claims in the Antarctic

Although people live there year-round, there are no permanent inhabitants in the Antarctic. Seven countries claim **territories** in the Antarctic, but under the terms of the Antarctic Treaty of 1959, all claims south of 60° south are suspended. Twenty-six countries have scientific bases in Antarctica. Argentina has six bases and is the only country to reinforce its claim by arranging to have children born there. They remain citizens of Argentina, not Antarctica.

The Reindeer Herders

The best-known native inhabitants of the Eurasian shores of the Arctic Ocean are the Saami, or Lapps. Once, they lived throughout the northern forests, but their territory was gradually reduced by the expansion of farming in Scandinavia. Now, they live inside the Arctic Circle, in the very northernmost parts of Russia, Finland, Sweden, and Norway, an area known as Lapland.

Saami life is based on the **migration** of reindeer. The Saami are pastoralists—an ancient way of life that involves traveling with their herds from winter pastures in the sheltered forests north and west, to summer feeding grounds on the open tundra. The seasonal journey may be several hundred miles, with two or three camping stops on the way. The owners of the bigger herds use airplanes or helicopters to move their families to the summer grounds, leaving a few herders to follow the migrating animals. As the herders travel, they hunt and gather food from the countryside, but the

Dressed in reindeer skin coats, women of the Nenet tribe sit on a sled as they watch reindeer races being held.

Saami's main source of food is their herds. The reindeer provide milk, meat, skins, and **sinews** for most of the Saami needs. A few Saami have developed a valuable export trade in reindeer meat.

A Saami tent has a hole in the top to let out the smoke from the family fire.

A few reindeer are trained to pull sleds and carry luggage or to act as leaders of the herd. The others are accustomed to being with people, but they are not really tame.

The Saami live in tents, which they carry with them as they follow the herds. A cone-shaped framework of poles supports a cover made of reindeer skins stitched together. The whole tent can then be folded and loaded onto one or more pack reindeer in a few minutes when it is time to move. Large families need a number of trained pack animals to carry enough tents for them all to live in.

Nuclear threat to the Saami

The accident at the Chernobyl nuclear power station in 1986 spread radioactive dust over a large part of Lapland, the home of the Saami. They and their herds suffered from the disaster, because the meat and milk of their animals were no longer fit to be used. It may be many years before the reindeer-herders can fully resume their traditional way of life.

Arctic Explorers

The first explorers of the Arctic Ocean were Vikings, from Norway, in the ninth century. The Vikings launched expeditions from their settlement in Iceland that took them to Greenland and North America, as well as to Novaya Zemlya, off the north coast of Russia. Unfortunately, like the sealers many years later, they kept their discoveries secret, and their knowledge of the Arctic was not preserved.

More than 700 years later, Dutch and English explorers began to search for the "northeast passage"

The death of Franklin

In 1845, Sir John Franklin was sent by the British government with two ships, HMS *Erebus* and *Terror*, to seek the northwest passage. Franklin disappeared. In 1853, another expedition had news of him from Eskimo people, who had relics of his party, but this was not enough for Franklin's widow, Lady Franklin. She paid for yet another expedition in 1859, which found the bodies of many of the crew on King William Island, where they lie to this day. Records of the expedition, found at Victory Point, proved that Franklin had found the northwest passage.

Above: Captain Robert Peary claimed to have reached the North Pole in 1909, but there has always been some doubt about this claim.

Left: Fridtjof Nansen designed this ship, the Fram, *to survive being trapped in the Arctic ice. From 1893–96 it drifted with the ice across the Arctic Ocean.*

—a route from the Atlantic Ocean to the Far East. In 1553, Richard Chancellor landed at what is now Archangel and traveled overland to Moscow before returning to England. He learned that Russian sailors had been using the same route to reach Europe for more than fifty years.

The Dutch established a trading post at Archangel in 1565, but in spite of heroic attempts, they never reached beyond the Barents Sea. By 1600, the Russians had a trade route to western Siberia, and in 1645 they were sailing regularly along the north coast as far as the Kolyma River. The first European to sail through the Bering Strait, in 1648, was Captain Semyon Dezhnyov, around the cape that now bears his name.

A similar search went on for the "northwest passage," a route to the Far East across the top of North America, at about the same time. Frobisher and Davis, Weymouth, Hudson and Baffin were British explorers whose names are now on the map, but none of them succeeded in finding the northwest passage. The first to make the journey was Robert McClure, who started from the Pacific in 1850. His ship was trapped in the ice for two years north of Banks Island and finally rescued in 1854 by an expedition that brought him home by the eastward route.

In 1969, the American ship *Manhattan* smashed through 620 miles of ice from Baffin Bay to Point Barrow, but the effort required was so great that the northwest passage may never be a regular trade route.

TRAVELERS IN POLAR WATERS
Exploring the Antarctic Ocean

The earliest sailors to see land in the Antarctic were not actually looking for it—they were blown off course from the area of Cape Horn, at the tip of South America. The first was a London merchant, Antoine de la Roche, in 1675, who anchored his ship in a fiord at the southern end of South Georgia. In 1739, the Frenchman Bouvet de Lozier discovered the tiny island that now bears his name, almost due south of the Cape of Good Hope. In 1756, sailors on the ship *Leon* also sighted South Georgia.

The tales of icebergs, seals, and penguins brought back by these first wanderers inspired a French and a British expedition in 1772. The French party, led by Yves de Kerguelen, turned back because of fog and bad weather. The leader of the British expedition was Captain James Cook,

In 1839–43 James Ross made two voyages into the Antarctic ice, in appalling weather. He discovered the sea and the ice shelf that are named after him.

with his two ships HMS *Resolution* and HMS *Adventure*. Cook claimed South Georgia for Great Britain and reported many seals and whales. Soon afterward, seal hunters followed Cook's directions to South Georgia and began exploring and sealing along the Antarctic Peninsula. Sealers discovered many new territories but added little to the knowledge of the area because they liked to keep their sealing grounds secret from their rivals. As a result, although the seals were nearly extinct by 1830, very few people knew where they came from.

From 1839–43, James Clark Ross, from Great Britain, explored the other side of the continent. In 1897, an expedition led by the Belgian explorer, de Gerlache, landed in several places along the Peninsula and became the first to spend the winter in Antarctica, when their ship was frozen into the ice in March 1898. They escaped almost a year later.

Gradually, the knowledge gained by explorers was put together with reports from sealers and whalers, until the great Antarctic Ocean and its islands were fully mapped.

The Russian research ship, Academik Fedorov, specially strengthened for ice breaking, supplies bases around the Antarctic coast.

Transportation in Polar Waters

In the Arctic, the northeast passage today is known as the Northern Sea Route, and it is in regular use. The passage is kept open throughout the year by a fleet of twenty **ice-breakers**. The biggest of these can cut through 6.5 feet of ice at 10 mph. The route allows millions of tons of **freight** to be carried between the ice-free Arctic port of Murmansk, on the Barents Sea, and Vladivostok, on the Pacific coast. Few ships make the whole passage. Most of them sail from one end of the route to ports in between, on the great rivers of Siberia. Eastward, freight is mainly fuel and general cargo, while timber and metal ores are brought westward out of Siberia.

Right: Most Alaskan seaplanes are small, with a single engine, but larger aircraft are used to carry heavier loads between island settlements.

Below: Leaving the harbor of Jakobshavn in West Greenland, a freighter begins its regular voyage to Denmark.

The northwest passage is not used so frequently. Its western end carries supplies to industrial settlements, including mines and oil fields in Alaska and the Canadian **Archipelago**. Ownership of the route is claimed by Canada, which expects other nations to ask permission before crossing, but few ships attempt the difficult journey all the way to the east.

Most transportation in Arctic regions is now by air, mainly small **seaplanes** traveling between island settlements. Thousands of people cross the Arctic Ocean every day, most of them without realizing it—the **Great Circle routes** between Europe and the West Coast of the United States pass within 500 miles of the North Pole.

The struggles to find routes around the Arctic Ocean were not repeated in the Antarctic, although some of the first accidental explorers were merchants blown off course as they tried to round Cape Horn. Since the Panama Canal was opened, in 1914, sailors who round the Horn make the voyage because of the challenge, not because they have to. Apart from scientific research vessels and fishing boats, the only ships sailing in Antarctic waters today are tourist ships making summer cruises in this spectacular part of the world.

RESOURCES OF THE POLAR REGIONS
Treasures of the Arctic

The Arctic covers 8 percent of the earth and contains 15 percent of its land area, so the region is likely to contain a considerable amount of mineral resources. So far, there has been little exploration of these resources, partly because conditions are so difficult. The principal resources exploited today are **hydrocarbons**.

Two of the world's major sources of oil and natural gas are in the Arctic. Siberia contains an area 500 mi. wide and 750 mi. from north to south that produces most of Russia's oil and gas. In the West, the North Slope of Alaska produces 20 percent of U.S. oil output, but only 11 percent of what the country uses. Smaller but significant centers of oil production are in the Northwest Territories of Canada and in other parts

Right: Logging operations in the Arctic, where ancient forests are felled for high-grade timber, have become the subject of controversy. Once cleared, the forests will take centuries to recover.

Below: Barentsberg, a Russian coal-mining station in Svalbard, is one of the most northerly permanent settlements in the world.

of Russia. Mineral exploration is continuing, and further sites will probably be discovered, especially on the wide continental shelf under the Eurasian Basin. In Alaska, the Alaskan National Wildlife Refuge (known as ANWAR) is the subject of a fierce argument between **environmentalists**, who want it preserved, and the petrochemical industry, who want to drill there for oil.

Coal has been mined in Svalbard, north of Norway, since 1900, and there may still be enough coal under the Arctic to last for 600 years. However, the coal is expensive to mine, and mining efforts in Russia have concentrated more on high-value minerals such as diamonds, platinum, gold, tin, and copper. Copper is also mined in Alaska, but not in large amounts, and the lead and zinc found there can be mined more cheaply elsewhere.

All over the Arctic, especially in Siberia, the growth of mining and oil-drilling since the 1950s has had a marked effect on the native peoples. Timber felling has resulted in improved communications, so people who have lived in isolation for thousands of years are suddenly feeling the impact of other cultures.

The pipeline carrying oil from Alaska to tankers for export

Hidden Treasures of the Antarctic

Knowing that the Antarctic continent was once part of the ancient supercontinent of Gondwana, **geologists** have been able to work out which parts were connected to which other continents. Comparing what can be seen from the surface with what is known about similar places in South Africa, for example, they have been able to find places in Antarctica that should be similar underground. One such place is called the Dufek Massif, about halfway to the South Pole from the shore of the Weddell Sea. To geologists, it looks like the Bushveld Complex, in South Africa, which is the source of 85 percent of the world's platinum.

However good this theory may be, the practical problems of **prospecting** for platinum under thousands of feet of ice,

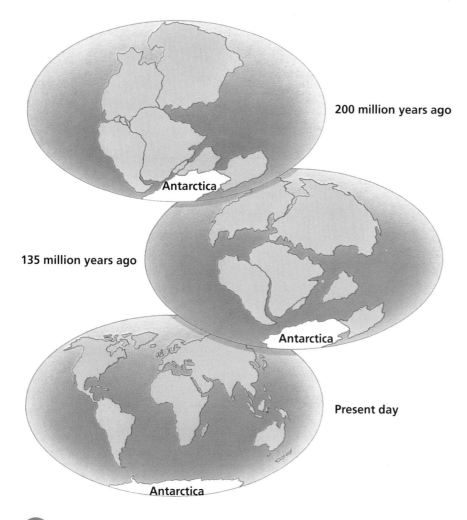

200 million years ago

Antarctica

135 million years ago

Antarctica

Present day

Antarctica

Over a period of millions of years, the world's continents have moved. Places where Africa and South America used to be attached to Antarctica may offer clues to the secrets of Antarctic rocks. Minerals present in continents that were once joined to Antarctica may also be present in Antarctica.

Above: A geologist obtaining rock samples in Antarctica. Samples of valuable minerals have been found in this region, but it is difficult to establish how much more might be found.

350 mi. from the nearest sea, make it very unlikely that the Dufek Massif will ever be mined.

In the same way, there is known to be high-grade coal under Antarctica, beside the shores of the Ross Sea, and some of poorer quality, together with iron ore, in the Prince Charles Mountains. But the expense and difficulty of mining it would make it completely uneconomical. All over Antarctica, geologists have found traces of minerals, but there is no evidence to suggest that any of them exist in quantities that would be worth mining.

Although Antarctic mineral exploitation is unlikely in the near future, a number of countries have worked together to endorse the Madrid Protocol, which is part of the Antarctic Treaty. Under this rule, all mineral activity is banned except for research. This may prove to be a sensible control, because we have no way of knowing what new technologies may be invented to extract Antarctica's hidden treasures or what value future generations may place on them.

Wealth from the Sea

The plentiful supply of food in polar waters supports large fisheries, both in the Arctic and the Antarctic. The Arctic is responsible for 10 percent of the world's fish catch, but some species, such as cod and halibut, are now so overfished that their populations may be in danger of collapsing. Periodic "fish wars" between the nations involved show that they all recognize the danger. Cooperation to protect the fish stocks is the only way forward, but competition between the fishing countries has so far got in the way.

The lakes and rivers of the Arctic tundra, both in Canada and Russia, provide freshwater fish such as wild salmon and Arctic char. There is also a small but profitable market in flying these delicacies south where people are prepared to pay high prices for them.

Some fishing practices are more destructive than others. Small-scale activities, such as longline fishing for cod in Greenland, do no lasting harm to fish stocks.

Large-scale "industrial" fishing efforts from overseas may soon put small Greenland fishermen out of business by ruining the fish populations.

Overfishing is even more serious in the Antarctic, where as one species is overfished, the fishermen turn their attention to the next. When whaling began at South Georgia in 1904, the whalers commented on the large numbers of fish around the island, but it was not until the late 1960s that commercial fishing started. In 1967–68, the catch was only a few hundred tons. But in the following season it was 90,000 tons, and a year later it peaked at 400,000 tons and then fell dramatically. A similar pattern was seen in other areas, as the fleet moved on. Between 1970 and 1990, the total catch from Antarctic waters was 5.5 million tons. By world standards this is not very big, but because Antarctic fish grow and mature so slowly, overfishing may have done long-term damage to fish populations. It may also have harmed populations of fish-eating birds and seals, especially near their breeding islands. Fishing for squid and krill, too, may have a serious effect on the animals that depend on them for food.

The History of Whaling

Whaling began in **temperate** waters, when coastal people killed passing whales for food. It moved to the Arctic as a commercial operation in the sixteenth century. At that time, large whales were common, unafraid, and easy to kill. By 1680, the Dutch whaling base on Svalbard had grown into a small town. As whales became scarce, the whalers had to travel farther to find them. In America, in 1614, whales were caught from the shore, but by 1760, hunters had to go to the Gulf of the St. Lawrence to find them. By the early 1800s, when the American whaling industry was properly established, whalers from Nantucket and New Bedford were sailing deep into Arctic waters. Later, in the mid-nineteenth century, they had to sail to Hawaii to find enough whales to justify the voyage.

Whales were occasionally killed in Antarctic waters, but southern whaling really started in 1904, when a station was

Right: The old whaling station at Grytviken in South Georgia is disused and rusting away, but the populations of great whales may never recover.

Below left: Admiration of whale hunters for their bravery has given way to dismay at the unnecessary slaughter of whales for food that is not really needed.

Below: Fur seals on South Georgia. Now that they are no longer hunted, their population has recovered rapidly.

opened on South Georgia. By 1914 there were six whaling stations in the area, with twenty-one **factory ships** and sixty-two catching boats. The industry grew until 1930, when forty British and Norwegian factory ships produced so much whale oil that the market collapsed. After that, a **quota** system was introduced that was supposed to protect the whale stocks, although its real purpose was to limit the amount of oil produced in order to keep the price up.

Eventually, under the guardianship of the International Whaling Commission, more species were protected, and today there is almost no whaling at all. Whales are only allowed to be killed for scientific purposes, except by Arctic native peoples who can take a limited number each year. Japan is the only country still killing whales on the high seas. Whatever their scientific intentions, there are restaurants in Tokyo that serve whale meat as a special, and very expensive, delicacy.

ENVIRONMENTAL IMPACTS
People and Pollution

Pollution affects both polar regions, although it takes slightly different forms. The Arctic Ocean, surrounded by developed countries, has been polluted for many years, from the air and from the sea. Industries around its shores create air pollution, including the gases that cause acid rain. Even so, it is still cleaner than most places on Earth.

When the Antarctic supply ship, *Bahaia Paraiso*, sank in the Bismarck Strait in 1989, it spilled diesel oil and gasoline into the sea. Similar wrecks in the north, such as the *Exxon Valdez* in Alaska in the same year, showed that oil spills in cold water last longer than elsewhere in the world. In polar conditions, oil breaks down 100 times more slowly than in temperate waters.

A decaying memorial

One of the places of pilgrimage for visitors to the Antarctic is Captain Scott's hut at Cape Evans, on the shore of the Ross Sea. The cold has preserved the hut, and all its associated artifacts, in perfect condition since Scott's death on the way back from the South Pole in 1912. In 1958 a party from HMS *Endeavour* cleared up the empty tins and seal carcasses left around it by later expeditions that had used it for shelter, and established it as a memorial to the great explorer. However, the breath and the body warmth of numerous visitors in recent years have caused it to start decaying.

Above: Early attempts to reduce pollution in the Antarctic included special incinerators designed to trap the ash from burning garbage.

The Antarctic has no industry, but it has always been affected by atmospheric conditions elsewhere in the world. Cores of ice taken from glaciers in the Antarctic show rising levels of carbon dioxide since the Industrial Revolution. With more people working in the Antarctic, it is vulnerable to more direct forms of pollution, particularly from oil.

Another long-lasting chemical found in Antarctic waters is a pesticide called DDT. Although this **pesticide** has never been used in the Antarctic, it has spread there from the rest of the world. The Antarctic Ocean shows the amount of pollution affecting the whole Earth.

All forms of human refuse last longer in icy conditions. The garbage from oil exploration in the Arctic and research bases in the Antarctic must now be removed, instead of being dumped into the sea or stacked on the ice and disposed of in warmer climates.

Left: Immortal garbage: these plastic drums will last for centuries in Antarctic conditions.

Ice persists in polar regions because of its ability to reflect sunlight. If the surface is darkened by pollution, the ice will melt faster. This could make the sea levels rise, causing flooding in coastal cities, and possible changes to the earth's climate.

The Hole in the Sky

Ozone is a poisonous gas formed by the action of sunlight on oxygen. Instead of two oxygen atoms, ozone gas contains three. At ground level, when it develops as part of the smog caused by sunshine on traffic pollution, ozone is very dangerous. High in the **stratosphere**, however, ozone absorbs the sun's harmful ultraviolet (UV) rays, protecting all forms of life. Without this shield, UV harms animals and plants and can cause skin cancer in humans. If the ozone layer becomes thinner, the amount of UV reaching the earth's surface increases.

Since 1957, British scientists at Halley Station, off the Weddell Sea area of the Antarctic, have been measuring the amount of ozone in the stratosphere, 12.5 miles above the ground. In 1981 they noticed that the level in spring was falling steadily. It fell by 30 percent in the next ten years, and in 1993 the lowest level ever recorded was 70 percent less than it was in the 1960s.

The cause of the reduction in ozone is a group of chemicals called chlorofluorocarbons (CFCs). These chemicals were

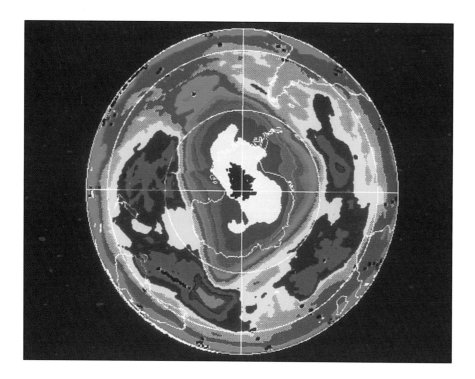

The hole in the ozone layer is measured by satellite photographs. In this image, the concentration of ozone is represented by colors—the pale pink patch in the middle is the "hole in the sky."

developed for use in **aerosols** and plastic foams and as the cooling agent in refrigerators and air conditioners. The chemicals are very stable, taking at least 100 years to break down in the air. This happens when they float high above the stratosphere, where sunlight causes them to release atoms of chlorine. Each chlorine atom sinks into the ozone layer, splitting the three-atom molecules into ordinary oxygen. The chlorine is not used up in this reaction, so each atom can go on to destroy up to 100,000 ozone molecules.

The way to stop this destruction is clearly to stop using CFCs. But because the chemicals last for so long, it will be a long time before the ozone layer will be able to renew itself.

Atmospheric conditions can be measured by meteorological balloons, which carry packages of instruments high into the sky, sending back information by radio.

ENVIRONMENTAL IMPACTS
Oil in the Far North

Drilling for oil is expensive and can be very messy, but because the whole world depends on oil for transportation and power, the drilling has to carry on. When an oil well "blows," it can spread pollution over a wide area. This was demonstrated in the Gulf War of 1991, when hundreds of oil wells were deliberately opened. Since wells blow in the normal course of events, ways of controlling them have been developed to lessen the damage.

Transporting oil is a different matter. On the North Slope of Alaska, a large oil field produces about a fifth of U.S. output. From Prudhoe Bay, a pipeline runs 800 miles south to Valdez, at the top of Prince William Sound. The pipeline has to be protected from breakage and heated to keep the oil flowing in cold weather. It is raised on stilts, to avoid interfering with the migration of the herds of caribou whose range it crosses.

Above: Killer whales were among the victims of the Prince William Sound oil spill. They suffered from inhaling the fumes and from eating fish poisoned by the oil.

Left: After the wreck of the Exxon Valdez in 1989, floating booms (inflated pipes) were put out to try to control the spilled oil, but the damage was still terrible.

The unsolved problem lies between Valdez and the terminals from which the oil is distributed. It has to be carried by sea.

The wreck of the tanker *Exxon Valdez* in 1989 showed the dangers of carrying oil across water. Modern tankers are designed with double **hulls** to reduce the risk of spillage in an accident, but too many of these huge oil carriers were built before present regulations were enacted. These tankers are too expensive to be scrapped and are still used.

The damage caused by oil anywhere in the ocean is serious, because it poisons marine life and interferes with fisheries. In cold polar waters it is even more harmful, because it breaks down so slowly. Especially in polar regions, the transportation of oil by sea is a long-term problem waiting to be solved.

43

ENVIRONMENTAL IMPACTS
The Antarctic Treaty

Antarctica was discovered toward the end of the time when new lands were immediately exploited by their discoverers. Two factors saved it from the fate of, say, South Africa, North America, or Alaska. It was hard to get to and offered no immediate evidence of great riches. (The riches of the sea, seals and whales were stripped away as fast as current technology allowed.)

In 1948, fearing political upheavals over Antarctica, the United States proposed unsuccessfully that Antarctica should be ruled either by a group of eight nations or by the United Nations. In 1958, they suggested that Antarctica should be set aside for scientific research, under a treaty signed by all twelve nations that had bases there. The Antarctic Treaty was duly drawn up and signed on December 1, 1959. It covered all land and ice shelves south of latitude 60° south, leaving the high seas to international law.

These flags at the South Pole represent some of the countries that have signed the Antarctic Treaty since 1959.

Membership of the Antarctic Treaty

Founder Members and Consultative Parties
Argentina, Australia, Chile, France, New Zealand, Norway, and the United Kingdom claimed territory; Belgium, Japan, South Africa, the former U.S.S.R., and the United States signed, but had no claims at the time.

Other Consultative Parties
Brazil, China, Ecuador, Finland, Germany, India, Italy, Netherlands, Peru, Poland, Republic of Korea, Spain, Sweden, and Uruguay.

Other Signatories
Austria, Bulgaria, Canada, Colombia, Cuba, Czech Republic, DPR of Korea, Denmark, Greece, Guatemala, Hungary, Papua New Guinea, Romania, Slovak Republic, Switzerland, and Ukraine.

Since 1959, thirty more nations have joined. Their governments represent 80 percent of the world's population. The treaty has been expanded to improve the original wording and to cover situations that were unforeseen when it was first drawn up. In 1978, for example, a separate agreement was enacted to protect seals on the high seas, and in 1982 another to conserve all living marine resources. Agreements about minerals and CFCs have also been added. Further recommendations have been accepted from all the interested parties, to cover such factors as safety, tourism, and the exchange of information.

Antarctica is the last great wilderness on Earth, and it is humanity's last chance to defend an undisturbed part of the planet. The effort is worth doing, not just for its own sake, but to protect the climate of the world and the fate of plants and animals everywhere, including people.

The U.S. research base at McMurdo Sound. Scientists from many countries in the world come to Antarctica to carry out research.

Glossary

aerosols Substances sprayed from containers under pressure.

archipelago A group of islands.

astronomical Concerned with the study of the stars, including the sun.

baleen A type of whale with filters, instead of teeth, to catch food.

climate The weather conditions of a region.

constellation The apparent pattern made by a group of stars.

continental shelf A shallow underwater area, at the edge of a continent.

cordillera A chain of mountains.

core samples Cylinders of rock or ice, cut out with a special drill.

ecosystems All the plants and animals that live together in particular habitats.

environmentalists Groups of people who try to protect the environment.

factory ships Large ships where fish or whales are brought by smaller ships that have caught them. Factory ships freeze the fish.

freight A ship's cargo.

geologists Scientists who study the formation of the earth's crust.

Great Circle routes The shortest distances between two places on the globe, different from a straight line on a flat map.

gyre A circular current system.

hydrocarbons Fossil fuels such as oil or natural gas.

icebreakers Ships with specially strengthened hulls, so they can break through ice without being damaged.

ice caps The deep covering of ice over land or on mountaintops.

Inuit Native people of northern Siberia, Alaska, Canada, and Greenland.

krill Small, shrimplike creatures.

mammals A group of animals that have fur or hair, whose females give birth to live young.

migration A regular journey from one region to another.

outboard motors Portable motors, attached to the backs (sterns) of small boats.

pesticide A chemical used to kill pests.

plankton Small plants and animals that float in water.

plates Great slabs of rock, forming the earth's crust.

predators Animals that hunt other animals for food.

prey Animals hunted by other animals for food.

prospecting Exploring a region for traces of a particular mineral.

quota A limited amount.

salinity The amount of salt dissolved in water. Salinity is measured in parts per thousand.

seaplanes Planes that can take off and land on water.

sinews The strong material that connects muscles to bones.

springtails Small, wingless insects that jump using a springlike extension of their tails.

stratosphere The upper layer of the atmosphere, starting six miles above the earth.

temperate A warm climate.

territories Areas of land, often controlled by a government or ruler.

tree line A boundary beyond which it is too cold for trees to grow. The tree line may be around polar regions or on mountains.

tundra The area of the Arctic where the subsoil, below 12 in. deep, is permanently frozen.

Further Information

BOOKS TO READ:

Aldis, Rodney. *Polar Lands*. New York: Macmillan Children's Group, 1992.

Alexander, Bryan and Cherry Alexander. *Inuit*. Austin, TX: Raintree Steck-Vaughn, 1992.

Bonner, Nigel. *Polar Regions*. Habitats. New York: Thomson Learning, 1995.

Bullen, Susan. *The Arctic and its People*. New York: Thomson Learning, 1995.

Byles, Monica. *Life in Polar Lands*. New York: Scholastic Inc., 1993.

Stonehouse, Bernard. *Snow, Ice, and Cold*. Repairing the Damage. New York: Macmillan Children's Group, 1993.

Taylor, Barbara. *Arctic and Antarctic*. Eyewitness. New York: Dorling Kindersley Publishing, 1995.

CD ROMS:

Geopedia: The Multimedia Geography CD-Rom. Chicago: Encyclopedia Britannica.

Habitats. Austin, TX: Raintree Steck-Vaughn, 1996.

USEFUL ADDRESSES:

Center for Environmental Education, Center for Marine Conservation, 1725 De Sales Street NW, Suite 500, Washington, DC 20036

Earthwatch Headquarters, 680 Mount Auburn Street, P.O. Box 403, Watertown, MA 02272-9104

Index